www.mascotbooks.com

For more information, please contact:
Mascot Books
560 Herndon Parkway #120
Herndon, VA 20170
info@mascotbooks.com

CPSIA Code: PRT0913A
ISBN-10: 1620862948
ISBN-13: 9781620862940

Printed in the United States

THAT'S NOT OUR MASCOT?

Bully™ is Our Mascot

by **Jason Wells and Jeff Wells**

illustrated by Patrick Carlson

That's not our mascot...

it's Albert, the Florida Gator.

Who's that batting
in Polk-DeMent Stadium?

That's not our mascot...
it's Hairy Dawg,
the Georgia Bulldog.

Who's that leading
the Dawg™ Walk?

That's not our mascot...
it's Scratch, the Kentucky Wildcat.

MISSISSIPPI STATE™

Who's that ringing the Cowbells?

MISSISSIPPI STATE ™

That's not our mascot...

it's Big Al, the Alabama Elephant.

That's not our mascot... it's Rebel, the Ole Miss Black Bear.

Who's that working out at the Sanderson Center?

Who's that dancing at the Bulldog™ Bash?

Who's that studying at
Mitchell Memorial Library?

That's not our mascot...
it's Smokey, the Tennessee Volunteer.

Who's that visiting the Chapel of Memories?

That's not our mascot...
it's Mr. C, the Vanderbilt® Commodore.

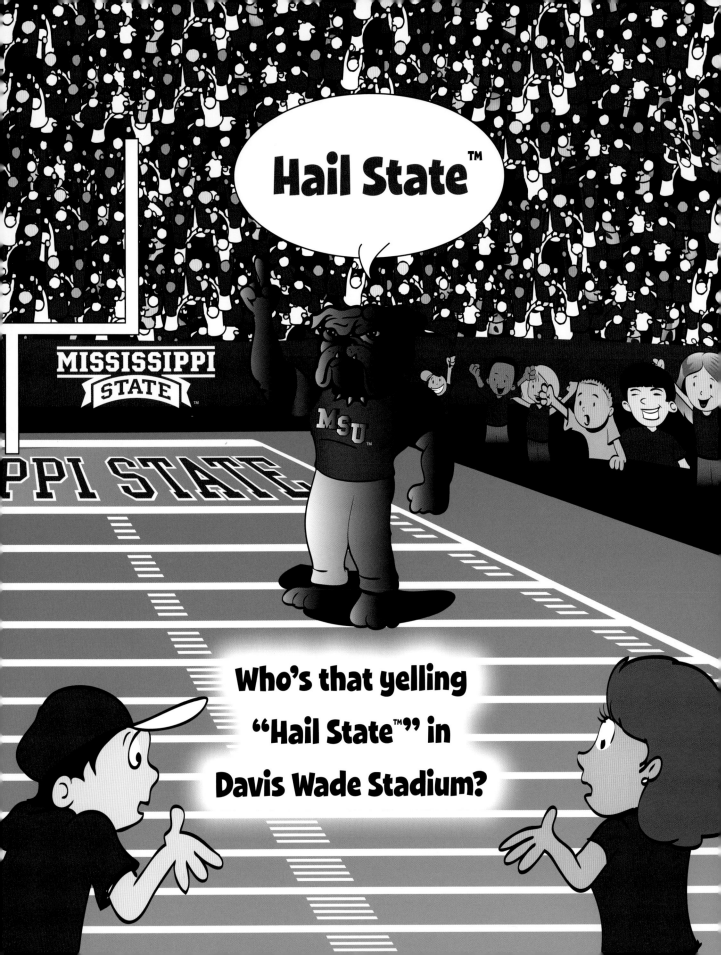